ERIC CARLE
Walter the Baker

READY-TO-READ

SIMON SPOTLIGHT
New York   London   Toronto   Sydney   New Delhi

This book was previously published with slightly different text.

For my mother and father

SIMON SPOTLIGHT

An imprint of Simon & Schuster Children's Publishing Division

1230 Avenue of the Americas, New York, New York 10020

Copyright © 1972, 1985 by Eric Carle

Eric Carle's name and signature logo type are registered trademarks of Eric Carle.

First Simon Spotlight Ready-to-Read edition 2014

For information about special discounts for bulk purchases, please contact Simon & Schuster Special Sales at

1-866-506-1949 or business@simonandschuster.com.

The Simon & Schuster Speakers Bureau can bring authors to your live event. For more information or to book an event

contact the Simon & Schuster Speakers Bureau at 1-866-248-3049 or visit our website at www.simonspeakers.com.

Manufactured in the United States of America 0414 LAK

First Edition 10 9 8 7 6 5 4 3 2 1

Library of Congress Cataloging-in-Publication Data

Carle, Eric.

Walter the Baker / Eric Carle. — First edition.

pages cm. — (Ready-to-read. Level 2)

"First Simon Spotlight Ready-to-Read edition."

Originally published in a slightly different form by Knopf in 1972.

Summary: By order of the Duke, Walter the Baker must invent a tasty roll through which the

rising sun can shine three times.

[1. Bakers and Bakeries—Fiction. 2. Pretzels—Fiction.] I. Title.

PZ7.C21476Waj 2014

[E]—dc23

2013030570

ISBN 978-1-4814-0917-9 (pbk)

ISBN 978-1-4814-0918-6 (hc)

This book was previously published with slightly different text.

Long ago, in a town encircled by a
wall, lived Walter the Baker,
his wife Anna, and their son Walter Jr.

Walter the Baker was known
even outside the walls of the town.
He was the best baker in the whole
Duchy.

Early every morning, while
everybody else was still asleep,
Walter began baking his breads,
rolls, cookies, tarts, and pies.

Anna sold the baked goods in the store.

No one could resist the warm, sweet
smells drifting from Walter's bakery.
People came from near and far to
taste the delicious rolls.

The Duke and Duchess who ruled
over the Duchy loved Walter's
sweet rolls. Every morning Walter Jr.
carried a basketful of warm sweet rolls
to the castle where they lived.

"Mmm," said the Duchess,
    spreading jelly on her roll.

"Ahh," said the Duke,
   putting honey on his.
   And so each day was
   the same as the day before—
   until one early morning . . .

... when Walter's cat was chasing
a mouse and tipped over the can of milk.

"What will I do?" cried Walter.
"I cannot make sweet rolls without
fresh milk."
Walter grabbed a pitcher of water.
"I hope nobody will notice the
difference," he said as he poured the
water into the flour to make the dough.

Now, you and I may not be able
to tell the difference between a roll
made with water and one made with
milk. But the Duke and especially
the Duchess could tell the difference.
"Ugh," cried the Duchess after she
took a bite.

"What is this!" roared the Duke.
"Where is Walter the Baker?
Bring him here at once!"

So Walter was brought before the Duke.
"What do you call this?" roared the Duke.
"This is not a roll, this is a stone!"
  And with that he threw it at
  Walter's feet.
"I used water instead of milk,"
  Walter admitted, hanging his head
  in shame.

"Pack your things and leave this town
 and my Duchy forever,"
 shouted the Duke. "I never want
 to see you again!"
"My Duke," pleaded Walter, "this is
 my home. Where will I go? Please
 give me one more chance, please."

The Duke remembered Walter's good
rolls and how much he and
the Duchess would miss them.

"You may stay—but only if you can
invent a roll through which
the rising sun can shine three times,"
said the Duke. "It must be made
from one piece of dough, and it must
taste good. Now go home and bring me
such a roll tomorrow morning."

Poor Walter! Worried and sad,
he trudged back to his bakery.

Walter worked all day and night.
He made long rolls, short rolls,
round rolls, and twisted rolls.
He made thin rolls and he made
fat rolls.

Walter beat, pulled, pushed,
and pounded the dough.

But it was all in vain.

He could not come up with a roll
that would please the Duke.
By early morning Walter had only
one long piece of dough left.
"It's hopeless," he cried.
In a sudden fit of anger, he grabbed
the last piece of dough and flung it
against the ceiling.

"Stick there!" he yelled at the dough.
But it didn't. It fell, twisting itself
as it dropped and plopped
into a pail of water.

Anna and Walter Jr. were awakened
by Walter's yell. They rushed
into the bakery just as Walter was
about to dump out the water
and the twisted
piece of dough.

"Father, stop!" shouted Walter Jr. "Look!"

Anna quickly popped the dough into the hot oven. Soon it was brown and crisp. She took out the roll and handed it to Walter. It hadn't risen very high, but it had three holes.

Walter held up the twisted roll and smiled. He saw that the morning sun was shining through it three times.

Walter put the roll into a basket
and rushed to the castle to deliver
his invention to the Duke and Duchess.

The Duke and Duchess saw
the morning sun shine through the roll
three times. Then they each took
a small bite. Walter was afraid
to look, because he had no idea
how it would taste.

"Well done!" said the Duke.
"Perfect!" exclaimed the Duchess.
They were both glad that Walter
would not have to be sent away.

And Walter too was happy that he could stay.

"Now, pray tell us. What
   do you call this?" asked the Duke.

"Uh, yes, pray us tell . . ."
   Walter stammered, as he tried
   to come up with a name.

"What was that? Pra . . . pre . . .
   pretzel?" said the Duke. "Pretzel
   it shall be. From now on, it shall be
   sweet rolls in the morning . . ."

". . . and pretzels in the afternoon,"
   said the Duchess.

Walter returned to his bakery and spent
all day and night making pretzels
for the whole town to taste.
The next morning everyone cheered
for Walter the Pretzel Maker.